Yes Days   No Days

To my Zen Masters, Kai and Riven.
With love and a great big YES, Mia.

First published in 2013 by Light Page Publishing.
16 – 11th Street Albertskroon, Johannesburg, South Africa 2195

Text copyright © Mia Von Scha Illustration copyright © Mirna Stevanovic

ISBN 978-0-9870027-3-0

I bounce out of bed
in the morning and I say,

"YES YES YES, it's another great day."

With a smile on my face
and a rainbow in my sky,

I feel so light I could almost fly.

The day I wake up on the wrong side of my bed
all I hear is "I hate this day"
running round my head.

With a frown on my face at the dumb rainbow,
my whole day is starting
with a "NO NO NO."

On the YES day
my breakfast is looking scrumdiddliyum

And I call out,
"Wow I love this food,
thanks my awesome mum!"
I devour each mouthful and I lick my chops,

my tummy's feeling yummy
and my day is looking tops.

On the NO day the same thing
looks like alien goo,

and I scrumple my face up
as I chew and chew and chew.

I give up and spit it out
and push my plate aside,

"I hate you mum!"
I shout as I storm outside.

On the YES day
the rain brings a sparkle to my eye,

as I rush outside and splash at everything that still looks dry.

"Isn't life so wonderful?" I screech and twirl around, landing with a giggle in a puddle on the ground.

On the NO day
the rain outside is looking pretty grim,

and I stay out there only because
I don't wanna go back in.

"You're ruining my life!"
I shout out, feeling rather bleak,

as the rain and my tears
roll together down my cheek.

My YES day afternoon is filled with lots of surprises:

A new puzzle, blowing bubbles, and dressing in disguises.

I call to my friend, "Having as much fun as me?"

As we scramble together up my favourite tree.

The NO
afternoon is a very dull affair:

A stupid puzzle, boring bubbles
and dressing like a bear.

"Get away from me!"
I call to the kid that's come to play,

as I climb up my tree alone
and hide there sulking all day.

When the YES day is over
and I'm snuggled in my bed,

thoughts of joy and happiness
are floating round my head.

I say, 'thanks for this day
and all the fun it's been',

and I can't wait to see
what will happen in my dreams.

When the NO day is over
it still comes with a fight:

my pillow isn't comfy
and my blanket's just not right.

I roll over crossly and say, "it's just not fair"

and I bet this day will end
with a horrible nightmare.

So if I wake tomorrow and see a NO day
coming on,

I'll stop it in its tracks and shout,
"Off with you 'NO', be gone!"

And I'll change it to a 'YES'
as quick as quick can be,

then I know that my whole day
will work out wonderfully

Because every day we have a choice between a YES and NO,

even if it's raining or our games don't seem to flow.

So every day when you wake up say, "YES YES YES"

to whatever life brings, and your day will be the best.